D0389387

The
ALPHABET
THIEF

Bill Richardson

PICTURES BY

Roxanna Bikadoroff

Groundwood Books
House of Anansi Press
Toronto   Berkeley

Groundwood Books / House of Anansi Press
groundwoodbooks.com

We acknowledge for their financial support of our publishing program the
Canada Council for the Arts, the Ontario Arts Council
and the Government of Canada.

 Canada Council   Conseil des Arts
for the Arts   du Canada

 ONTARIO ARTS COUNCIL
CONSEIL DES ARTS DE L'ONTARIO
an Ontario government agency
un organisme du gouvernement de l'Ontario

With the participation of the Government of Canada | Canadä
Avec la participation du gouvernement du Canada

Library and Archives Canada Cataloguing in Publication
Richardson, Bill, author
The alphabet thief / Bill Richardson ; Roxanna Bikadoroff, illustrator.
Issued in print and electronic formats.
ISBN 978-1-55498-877-8 (hardback).
— ISBN 978-1-55498-878-5 (PDF)
1. English language—Alphabet—Juvenile poetry. 2. Alphabet
books. I. Bikadoroff, Roxanna, illustrator II. Title.
PS8585.I186A67 2017   jC811'.54   C2016-905742-9
C2016-905743-7

The illustrations were done in ink and watercolor on paper.
Design by Michael Solomon
Printed and bound in Malaysia

To Bill Pechet — BR

To Maurice Sendak — RB

THE ALPHABET THIEF *was daring and smart.*
When the night was silent and black,
She stole all the letters, she gathered them up
And took them away in her sack.

The Alphabet Thief stole all of the A's,
And all of the coats became cots.
All of the fairs were turned into firs,
And all of the boats became bots.

The Alphabet Thief stole all of the B's,
And all of the bowls became owls.
All of the brats were turned into rats,
And when Bill became ill, how he howled.

The Alphabet Thief stole all of the C's,
And a cloud became loud in the sky.
My chair wasn't there — it had turned into hair —
And all of the spices were spies.

The Alphabet Thief stole all of the D's,
And every beard was a bear.
Cows found the dairy was suddenly airy,
And drains turned to rains everywhere.

The Alphabet Thief stole all of the E's,
And batches of bears became bars.
When lambs tried to bleat, the sound came out blat,
But no one could stare, only star.

The Alphabet Thief stole all of the F's,
And every fox was an ox.
The geese cried "Hooray!" when that cad went away,
But were shocked when their flocks became locks.

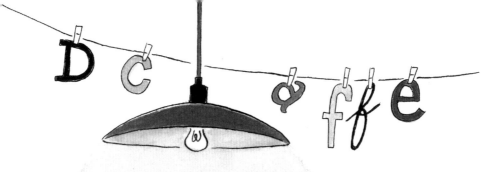

C<small>AN NOBODY STOP</small> *the Alphabet Thief?*
Can nobody end her spree?
Can somebody best her, can someone arrest her
Before she takes all of the G's?

The Alphabet Thief stole all of the G's,
And every finger was finer.
No one could tell how to knell on a bell,
Since dingers had now become diners.

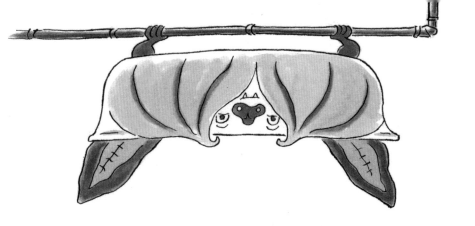

The Alphabet Thief stole every H,
And suddenly baths were all bats.
The hoboes were oboes, and cowboys discovered
Their favorite chaps were now caps.

The Alphabet Thief stole all of the I's.
The maid was made mad in a glance.
And artists at easels would rather have measles
Than find that their paints were now pants.

The Alphabet Thief stole all of the J's,
And ninjas surrendered their swords.
For ninjas were Ninas, and over in Norway,
Fjords were transformed into Fords.

The Alphabet Thief stole all of the K's,
And fishermen's pikes became pies.
My monkey was money, which wasn't that funny,
And skunks were now suns up on high.

The Alphabet Thief stole all of the L's,
And the seals disappeared in the seas.
You couldn't cry "Halt!" because halt became hat,
Nor plead, because pleas turned to peas.

THE ALPHABET THIEF, *the Alphabet Thief,*
She's not in the market for gems.
She's after our letters, and somebody better
Arrest her to save all the M's.

The Alphabet Thief stole all of the M's.
A hockey team turned into tea.
It spilled on the ice — ice that used to be mice —
And that's not the iced tea for me!

The Alphabet Thief stole all of the N's,
So oodles of noodles were gone.
And chess is a mess when your pieces are paws,
And you ought to be playing with pawns.

The Alphabet Thief stole all of the O's,
So orange was turned into range.
There's no rhyme for orange, which poets — now pets —
Agree is surpassingly strange.

The Alphabet Thief stole all of the P's,
So quickly that rapid was raid.
A pirate was irate, and Scots in a tizzy
All wondered where plaid had been laid.

The Alphabet Thief stole all of the Q's,
Concealing them where I can't tell.
As Q stands with U, and they're always together,
She gathered the U's up as well.
Queasy was easy, and squash became sash,
And the squad so sad in the dark.
So squally was Sally that Noah decided
To shepherd the quark to the ark.

The Alphabet Thief stole of all of the R's,
And beer became bee, we assume.
All horses were hoses and closets exploded
As every broom became boom.

THE ALPHABET THIEF, *the Alphabet Thief,*
Whatever can anyone do?
Unless we can find her and somehow confine her,
The S's will soon be gone too.

The Alphabet Thief stole every S,
So soil turned to oil by and by.
Creatures that hiss were compelled to say "Hi,"
And snowmen were now men — oh my!

The Alphabet Thief stole every T,
And now she could tease us with ease.
Bundles of twine were turned into wine,
And caps made of tweeds became weeds.

The Alphabet Thief went after the V's,
So Seven just couldn't be seen.
"Fie," blubbered Five with a tear in her eye
To a moose where vamoose should have been.

The W's fell to the Alphabet Thief
Without any stumbles or glitches.
The imps, who'd been wimps, were in stitches that witches
Unhitched from their brooms were now itches.

The X's were next — which meant they were net —
For the Alphabet Thief was still free.
The witch, now an itch, tried to mutter a hex,
But a hex, when it's X-less, is he.

Nothing is left but the Y's and the Z's.
It seems like a horrible dream.
Can nobody stop the Alphabet Thief?
I think I've come up with a scheme.
I'll take all the Y's, and I'll take all the Z's,
And I'll run to the top of the hill.
The Y's will be slingshots, the Z's will be ammo,
I'll see her and fire at will.

A halo of Z's encircles her head.
Such snoring has never been heard.
When I open her sack, the letters spring back
And hurry on home to their words.

THE ALPHABET THIEF, *the Alphabet Thief,*
Someone could catch her, that's clear.
And who was the hero who saved the day?
It was me! You can write my name here.